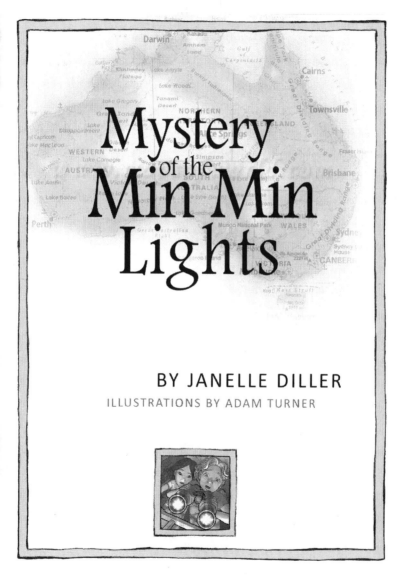

Mystery
of the
Min Min
Lights

BY JANELLE DILLER

ILLUSTRATIONS BY ADAM TURNER

Published by WorldTrek Publishing

Copyright © 2016 by Pack-n-Go Girls

Printed in the USA

Visit our website at www.packngogirls.com.

This is a work of fiction. Names, characters, places, and incidents either are the product of the author's imagination or are used fictitiously. The Australian outback is real, and it's a wonderful place to visit. Any other resemblance to actual events, locales, organizations, or persons, living or dead, is entirely coincidental and beyond the intent of either the author or the publisher.

Illustrations by Adam Turner

ISBN 978-1-936376-31-5

Cataloging-in-Publication Data available from the Library of Congress.

To Angela Lee for reminding me that *all* little girls should get to see themselves on the pages of the books they read.

Contents

Meet the Characters

Wendy Lee is spending six months in Australia. She's glad to meet Chloe and have a new friend.

Chloe Taylor loves their sheep station and can't wait to share it with Wendy.

Jack Taylor

is Chloe's brother. He
loves their dog, Buzz,
and climbing trees.

Buzz

is the best dog you
could ever hope to have
in the outback.

The Min Min Lights

are out there somewhere!

And now, the mystery begins . . .

Mystery of the Min Min Lights

Chapter 1

Moving Day

Wendy Lee watched the men carrying boxes into the tidy yellow house. Her mom stood in the shade of the wide front porch and directed the men. Wendy stood on a dry patch of grass and chewed her thumbnail. She knew she shouldn't bite her nails but couldn't help it. This was just one of those days.

"Hey! *G'day!*"

A squeaky voice from somewhere in the sky yelled at Wendy.

She twisted her head and looked up.

"'Ow yar goin'?" The voice squeaked again. Wendy had no idea what the voice said. None.

Wendy shaded her eyes against the sun. Holy smokes was it ever sunny. And hot. And dusty. The dry wind blew her straight black hair in tangles around her face. A fine layer of grit covered her teeth.

Wendy might have made a mistake to come to Australia with her mom. Maybe she should have stayed in San Francisco with her grandparents. She didn't know if she could take six month in this town. She squinted at the bright, cloudless sky and looked for where the voice came from.

A giant tree towered over the neighbor's yard. It looked, really, like a dozen trees all twisted together.

"Hey! You!" The tree seemed to be calling to her. "Whatcha' doin'? You movin' into that house?"

Finally. English. Sort of.

Moving Day

Wendy cocked her head and studied the branches. The noise seemed to come from two skinny legs wrapped around a thick tree branch. Wendy caught a glimpse of blond curls and a red sports jersey in between the broad emerald leaves.

"Wanna *chewie?*" the voice called down.

"Do I want to what?"

"A *chewie*," the voice said.

Wendy heard the leaves rustling.

"Catch!"

Wendy bit her nail again. She watched a small purple rectangle flutter down from the leaves.

"It's yummers. It's like blueberry," the voice said.

Wendy glanced around to see if her mom was looking in her direction. In San Francisco she would *never* eat something that a stranger gave her. Even if the stranger turned out to be a kid who sat in a tree. She picked up the purple paper, unfolded the wrapper, and stuck the candy in her mouth.

Gum. *Chewie* was gum. And it tasted just like the voice said. Blueberries.

This she liked! And then she sighed. She couldn't understand anything. This kid was talking English, but it wasn't like any English Wendy knew.

"Crikey!" Wendy proudly said the one word of Australian slang she'd learned from *Crocodile Hunter* shows.

"Crikey? Crikey?" the voice in the tree laughed wildly. "My granddad doesn't even say *crikey* anymore. *Crikey?"*

Wendy's face felt hot. She knew one word of Australian slang, and it turned out to be worthless. Worse than worthless.

Beyond the tree, a screen door slammed. "Jacko?" A girl about Wendy's age stepped out onto the wide wooden porch. She had lots of curly blond hair pulled back into a thick ponytail. Her tan arms and long legs matched the color of Wendy's skin. But the other girl got her color from being in the sun. The girl put her hands on her hips and huffed loudly. "Are you in the tree again, Jacko? Mum's gonna' be *cross as a frog in a sock* when she gets home."

No sound came from the tree. Even the leaves stopped rustling. Wendy saw the two skinny legs pull up onto the branch. She could still see the red jersey and the blond curls though.

"Jacko? I know you're up there." The girl trotted down the front steps and into the yard. She stopped at the trunk and looked up. A small purple rectangle appeared out of the leaves and landed on the ground. For the moment, Wendy couldn't see anything except the red shirt.

The girl picked up the gum, unwrapped it, and stuffed it in her mouth. "You can't bribe me with *lollies*, Jacko." She chewed loudly. "I'm still going to *dob on you* to Mum."

Another small purple rectangle dropped. The girl caught it and looked at it. She crammed it into her shorts pocket.

Wendy took a deep breath. "It's blueberry," she said. "We don't get that flavor of *chewies* in the US." Maybe the girl would think she was Australian. But probably not.

"Huh?" The girl turned and looked at her for the first time. "Who are you?"

Moving Day

Up close like this, Wendy liked how the girl looked even though she had lots of freckles. Her blue eyes matched the morning sky.

"I'm Lee Wen Chi," she said and used her Chinese name. Her heart thumped in her chest. She wasn't used to having to talk to strangers. "My friends call me Wendy. I'm from San Francisco, California. My mom's company sent her here to do a big software project for a huge mining company. She brought me along. I'm going to go to school here and everything."

Everything.

Wendy's stomach did a little somersault. She bit her nail again. What if this girl didn't like her? What if she didn't have any friends? What if she hated Australia? Six months felt like half her lifetime.

The girl tilted her head. She looked confused. "Why do you have two names?"

Wendy tried not to sigh. She wished she had told the girl only her American name. "Well, my mom was born in China and came to the US as a little girl. She's lived in the US a long time, but she still is kind of Chinese." Wendy knew that didn't make sense. But she didn't know how to explain it any other way. "She gave me a Chinese name so I wouldn't forget I'm Chinese. And she gave me an American name so I'd remember I'm American, too."

"Hummmm." The tan girl nodded. "Wen Chi and Wendy kind of sound the same."

"Exactly. The names are kind of the same and kind of different." That's how Wendy felt sometimes even in San Francisco. She was mostly American. But she was also still a little Chinese.

The other girl smiled a happy, toothy smile. "Well, Wendy Wen Chi, welcome to 'Stralia. My name's Chloe. I'm nine."

Moving Day

"Me, too!" Wendy said. "And you can just call me Wendy." She felt happier than she had all day. Well, except for when she got the piece of gum from the kid in the tree.

Above them, the boy's legs scraped against one tree branch and then another and then another. In a minute, the curly-haired boy in the red jersey swung off of the lowest branch and dropped to the ground.

"*G'day!* I'm Jack." He dusted his hands off on his shorts. "You got nice teeth."

Chloe rolled her eyes. "Don't pay any attention to him. He's going into *kindy* next year. He's a real *earbasher* he is."

"*Earbasher?*" Wendy repeated.

Chloe shrugged her shoulders and rolled her eyes again. "He talks nonstop." She gave her brother a fed-up big-sister look. "I'm going to tell Mum you were up in the tree again!" She shook her finger at him. "Just as soon as she gets home from the police."

"Police?" Wendy shifted her eyes from the girl to the boy and back to the girl.

Jack nodded. "They've got to catch the sheep *duffers*."

"*Duffers?* What's that?" Wendy asked.

"Thieves," Chloe said firmly. Her face looked grim.

"You mean people are stealing sheep?" Wendy asked. Her voice sounded squeaky. She bit her nail again.

Jack looked at his sister. "*Yeh*. Except it's not people who are doing it." He scanned the sky and then leaned close to Wendy. His voice dropped to a whisper. "It's UFOs."

Chapter 2

The Invitation

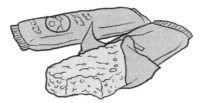

"Well, does she seem like a nice girl, Chi Chi?" Mrs. Lee asked Wendy. Her mom always used her Chinese nickname.

Wendy thought for a minute. They were eating dinner, except dinner was only a box of granola bars and water. Not even milk. Her mom wasn't exactly a great cook. And with all the moving stuff, she hadn't had time to go to the grocery store yet to pick up some deli food. Wendy suddenly worried the grocery store might not have a deli. She tried not to groan out loud.

"Yeah. She seems nice. And I think Jacko is kind of funny," Wendy said. She took another bite of the granola bar. At least her mom had packed the soft, chewy kind and not the crunchy kind. What would they eat when they ran out of granola bars? Then she had an even worse thought. What if her mom had six months of granola bars packed in one of their moving boxes? What if her mom never went to the grocery store again? She sighed.

"I really liked Mrs. Taylor when I came here to house hunt last month. That's the big reason I rented this place," her mom said. "It was nice of them to invite you to their sheep ranch tomorrow. So why don't you want to go with them?" Her shoulder-length black hair swung as she tilted her head.

Wendy shook her head. They both knew

"sheep ranch" wasn't what you called it.

"It's not a sheep ranch," Wendy said. She tried to think of what they would call it in the US. But she didn't know anyone who raised sheep in California.

"Whatever." Mrs. Lee crumpled up the wrapper of her granola bar and opened another one. At this rate, they'd run out of granola bars by the weekend. Unless her mom *had* stashed a big supply in a moving box. Wendy didn't know which one to hope for.

"It's a . . . a station. A sheep station."

"Okay. A sheep station." Mrs. Lee pulled her granola bar into two pieces. Her purple fingernails trapped a bit of the goo. She licked them clean. "I wish I had some peanut butter to dip this into," she said.

Wendy loved peanut butter. But she was secretly glad they didn't have peanut butter. Otherwise dinner would be a loaf of bread, a jar, and a knife for the next week. Worse, it would probably be white bread. Not even whole wheat.

"Why are you worried about going with them this weekend? The mining company president knows Mr. Taylor. Says he's a good *bloke*." She giggled a little when she said the word. "That means he's a good guy."

Bloke. Wendy tucked that word away to use later.

"I guess Mr. Taylor's family owns the station. The house here," Mrs. Lee tilted her head at the house next door, "is their town house."

"But what about the sheep thieves?" Wendy asked. "And what if it really is a UFO that's stealing the sheep?" She had worried about that all afternoon.

"UFOs? Really, Chi Chi?" Mrs.

14

The Invitation

Lee took a dainty bite. She scrunched up her nose. "How silly. I mean, who believes in flying saucers? And why would they steal sheep?"

Wendy didn't say anything. Mostly because she certainly did believe in flying saucers.

"You think Chloe seems nice, though, right?" Mrs. Lee said. "You had a ton of fun playing with her today, right? You think you'll be friends with her, don't you, Chi Chi? I think the sheep station trip sounds like fun."

"Yeah, we had a lot of fun."

"Enough fun that you think you'll like living in Australia for a bit?"

Wendy paused and thought. "Yeah. Yeah, I think so." And she did. With Chloe as a neighbor maybe she wouldn't be lonely here after all. Maybe it would be okay to be here for six months.

At least it would be okay if the UFOs didn't start stealing little girls, too.

Chapter 3

Alone in the Outback

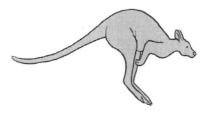

Wendy climbed in the dusty old red Land Cruiser and sat next to Chloe. Jack hopped into the front seat.

Mrs. Taylor started the car. "Boy, is it ever hot." Sweat ran down her freckled cheek. Her curly chestnut-colored hair stuck to her face. She turned on the air conditioner. Hot air blew out for the first few minutes.

"It's hot enough to fry an egg on a sidewalk," Wendy agreed. She wiped the sweat off her forehead.

"Sidewalk? What's that?" Jack asked.

"It's a *footpath*," Mrs. Taylor said.

"Huh? Don't you have a stove?" Jack asked.

"Stove? You have a stove?" Wendy acted surprised. "But then you probably have pans, too." She sighed. "Lucky dogs."

"What? You don't have a stove or pans?" Jack's eyes grew big. "I thought Americans were rich. You have two of everything. Cars, houses, TVs. Everything."

17

Mrs. Taylor laughed. *"She's 'aving a go."* And then she saw the confused look on Wendy's face. "You're teasing, right?"

Wendy nodded and laughed. And then so did Jack. "Okay. It's just that you Americans say the funniest things," Jack said.

They headed out of town on a smoothly paved highway. After an hour or so, they turned off onto a hard-packed red dirt road. The land looked scrubby and dry. And red. It reminded her of the trip she'd taken to Arizona with her *lao lao* and *lao ye*.

The thought of her grandparents made her throat thick. She missed them. She missed her *lao lao's* dim sum that she made for Wendy for an after school snack. She missed her *lao ye's* happy laugh. She could be with them right now in California instead of here in this hot, dusty place. But then she'd be missing her mom. Wendy stared out the window so Chloe wouldn't see the tears in her eyes.

Alone in the Outback

The sun dropped lower to the horizon. The land caught the evening colors of the sky. The reds grew redder. The oranges and yellows grew darker. It looked like a child's colorful painting. It made her feel a tiny bit better.

"Are we almost there?" Wendy figured they must be close to the sheep station to be on a road like this.

"Not far. Maybe about thirty *clicks*," Chloe said.

Mrs. Taylor looked at Wendy in the rearview mirror. "About thirty kilometers. That would be about eighteen miles, I think."

"On this road?" Wendy had never driven on a dirt road that far even when her *lao lao* and *lao ye* took her camping in Yosemite.

"It'll only be about another forty-five minutes," Mrs. Taylor said. "The homestead is in the middle of the station. The whole station is about 2,300 square kilometers." She tilted her head and thought a bit. "That would be about 900 square miles."

That sounded huge. But Wendy couldn't picture what she was talking about. It must have shown on her face.

Mrs. Taylor twisted her lip a bit. "That would be like if you had a square piece of land. Each side is thirty miles long. That's about how big the station is."

Wendy understood that enough to say "Wow!"

"Granddad used to run 30,000 sheep on his land," Chloe said. It didn't even sound like she was bragging. "Now we run only about 10,000."

"Less," Mrs. Taylor said. This time she kept her eyes on the road. But Wendy thought she heard her sigh. "We've had years of drought." She added, "No rain. It's been horrible."

"Still, that's amazing! You must have the biggest sheep station in all of Australia," Wendy said. "Maybe the world," she added.

"Oh no," Mrs. Taylor said. "There are lots of stations far bigger than ours. The biggest stations

are cattle stations. One is ten times the size of ours.
So that would be three hundred miles wide and
three hundred miles long."

"You're kidding! That's bigger than lots of the
states in the US," Wendy said.

Mrs. Taylor nodded. "Australia's a big country
with not very many people."

"Watch out! A *'roo!*" Jack yelled. An enormous
kangaroo leaped out of nowhere along side of
them.

"Aaaahhhhh!" the girls screamed at
the same time and grabbed each other's
arm.

Mrs. Taylor honked over
and over and slammed on
the brake. The kangaroo
bounded off in the
other direction. She
said something

under her breath and glanced in the rearview mirror. "Sorry. Don't tell your mum I said that." She stopped the car and wiped the palms of her hands on her legs.

Wendy laughed nervously. Her heart still pounded like crazy. "Was that a real kangaroo? I mean are we going to see more?" She couldn't believe she'd been *that close* to a real one.

"Oh yeah," Chloe said. "It's that time of the day. They're everywhere."

"Amazing! Wait till I tell my friends back in San Francisco. They all said to take pictures of the castles."

"Castles?" Chloe said. She sounded confused. "We don't have any castles in Australia."

"I know. All my friends kept getting Australia and Austria mixed up." What Wendy didn't say is that at first, she got them mixed up too. "They won't mix them up now. I wish I would have had my phone out to take a picture."

"A phone!" Jack said immediately. "You have your own phone? Can I have a phone, Mum?"

"Jacko, you're not going to get your own phone," Mrs. Taylor said and shook her head.

"It's my mom's old one," Wendy said and sighed. "It doesn't even work in Australia. But it still takes pictures. Will we see more kangaroos?"

"*No drama.* You don't have to worry." Mrs. Taylor said dryly. "We'll see plenty more."

"We just don't want to hit any," Jack added.

"Shush, Jacko," Mrs. Taylor and Chloe said at the same time.

"Well, we don't," Jack said.

"No. We need to keep our eyes peeled. It's starting to get dark, so they'll be out in full." She glanced at the sun dropping lower on the horizon. The sky colors mirrored the red, yellow, and orange colors of the land. "You kids keep watching out for more 'roos." She started the car and they took off down the road again.

Mrs. Taylor drove slower now. The three kids kept turning their heads to watch in every direction. Every now and then, one would shout, "There's one!"

As long as the kangaroos stayed away from the car, Wendy loved it. She pulled out her mom's old phone and took picture after picture after picture. It was like being in the middle of the kangaroo exhibit at the zoo. Only this was the real thing.

"Oh look!" Chloe squealed. "There's a joey. And another one."

The baby kangaroos hopped after their mothers. They almost looked like cartoon characters. *Boing, boing, boing.*

Mrs. Taylor would honk or slow down or speed up or sometimes swerve even though none of the kangaroos came close like the first one did.

In fact, the crazy thing was that it wasn't a

kangaroo at all they had to be afraid of. It was the snake on the road they needed to worry about. As soon as Mrs. Taylor saw it, she braked hard. The car skidded into a pothole. BANG! The tire blew. Mrs. Taylor limped the car to a stop.

"Now what?" Chloe asked nervously.

Wendy didn't like that Chloe sounded just like she felt. She bit her thumbnail.

Mrs. Taylor sighed. "I can see the lights to the station buildings from here. I'll run get another car. It can't be more than two or three *clicks* from here. The guys can change the tire in the morning when they don't have to worry about—" She glanced at the open bush around her. "I mean, when it's light."

"What do *we* do, Mummy?" Jack asked. His voice quivered a bit.

"You stay put in the car," Mrs. Taylor said. "This time of evening the snakes are still out and the dingoes are starting to come out. You'll be fine

right here." She grabbed a flashlight out of the glove compartment and opened her car door.

"But what if we see the Min Min lights?" Jack asked. His voice shook a little more.

"Min Min lights?" Wendy asked. She had no idea what kind of Australian slang this was. But the mention of them made everyone a little jittery. She could see that. She chewed her nail again.

Mrs. Taylor sighed. *"She's apples."*

"Apples? Who's apples?" Wendy asked. She had no idea why they were talking about apples.

Mrs. Taylor said, "I mean you'll be just fine." She added firmly, "Jacko, you won't see the Min Min lights."

"But what if we do?" Jack said again.

"Well, just don't get out of the car and let them grab you," she said. She slammed the car door and ran off into the dying light of the evening.

Chapter 4

The Min Min Lights

"What are the Min Min lights?" Wendy immediately asked. This didn't sound good AT ALL.

Chloe and Jack looked at each other. Their eyes darted around.

"They're lights that come out of nowhere at night. They can go fast or slow," Jack whispered. He twisted his neck back and forth as he looked in every direction.

"No one knows exactly what they are," Chloe

added in a hushed voice. She watched her mum jog up the road. Mrs. Taylor had turned on her flashlight, which showed a bouncing light ahead of her. Her thick curls flew up and down.

"I think they're UFOs," Jack said. "I think they're the ones stealing the sheep."

Wendy chewed on her nail. "The lights are UFOs? And they're stealing the sheep? You mean like a flying saucer or something from outer space?" What was she doing out here in the middle of nowhere? She scanned the horizon, but it was growing dark fast. She couldn't see much of anything except shadows and more shadows. Now for sure she wished she'd stayed in San Francisco. This seemed way too crazy.

Both Jack and Chloe nodded. "But we don't know. No one does," Chloe said. "The lights just appear when you're driving down the road. Sometimes they're behind you. Sometimes they're ahead of you. No matter how fast you go, you can't catch up to them."

"Some people chase them and then they just disappear," Jack said. He tried to snap his fingers.

"People disappear?" Wendy's heart pounded.

"No one ever sees them again," Chloe added. She nervously checked all four directions around the car.

Wendy looked from Chloe to Jack and back to Chloe again. And then she laughed nervously. "You're just pulling my leg."

Chloe and Jack looked confused. Jack looked at Wendy's leg. "Huh? We're not touching your leg."

Wendy tried again. "You're joking. You're—" What had Mrs. Taylor said? "You're *'aving a go*." That sounded kind of right.

Both of them stiffened. They shook their heads.

"It's the truth," Jack said.

"We wouldn't lie about this," Chloe said.

"It's *good oil*," Jack added.

The Min Min Lights

"Good oil?" Wendy asked.

"It means it's the truth," Chloe said. She looked very serious.

Something howled and the three of them jumped.

"Just a dingo," Chloe said.

Jack nodded fast. "Just a dingo."

"I don't think it's too close," Chloe added, but she scooted closer to Wendy and away from the window. Wendy scooted closer to Chloe, too.

"What are dingoes?" Wendy asked. She couldn't believe she had even more things to be afraid of.

"Dogs," Jack said.

"Wild dogs," Chloe said. "They can tear you apart."

"In the car?" Wendy asked. She felt desperate for a fast answer. "Are we safe in the car?"

"We're safe in the car," Chloe said. But she looked in every direction again. "From the dingoes at least."

Jack tumbled into the back seat. He squeezed

between the two girls. "I think we'll be okay if we stick together."

"I know the Min Min lights sound crazy, but it's true," Chloe said. "Our mum even saw them once."

"Your mum?"

Chloe and Jack nodded. "She was out on a long, empty stretch of road on a dark night," Chloe said. "At first she thought it was the moon, except there wasn't a moon that night. She said it chased

her for sixty *clicks*. She was really spooked by the time she got back to the house."

"And the *ringers* 've seen 'em too," Jack added. "Rex has seen a bunch of them."

"What's a *ringer?*" Wendy asked. "Who's Rex?"

"*Ringers* are the workers who help Dad run the station," Jack said.

"Rex is one of the foremen on the sheep station," Chloe said. "He's a *jackaroo*. So he's learning how to run the station. Sometimes we have a *jillaroo*. That's a girl *jackaroo*."

"Rex says they've been taking our sheep," Jack said.

At this, Chloe snorted and rolled her eyes. "Rex lies about everything."

"*Ridgy didge*. No he doesn't."

"Yes, he does. He said he wrestled a crocodile. And then he had the skin made into boots," Chloe said.

"Well he *does* have croc boots," Jack insisted.

"Yes, but he didn't *really* wrestle the croc they came from."

"Well I believe he wrestled *a* crocodile. And something *is* stealing the sheep," Jack said and looked at Wendy. "That's why Mum went to the police on Monday. But the police say they can't do anything. They can't just sit out here in the bush and watch for Min Min lights to show up and sheep to disappear."

Chloe nodded glumly. "But who knows if it's the Min Min lights?"

"What else could it be?" Jack insisted.

"Wait! What's that?" Wendy pointed down the road. An intense bright light zoomed straight toward them.

"AAAAHHHHH!" All three of them grabbed each other and screamed.

Chapter 5

Safe at Last

"Duck!" Wendy yelled.

"We're all gonna die!" Jack bellowed.

"Wait! I think . . . I think it's a . . . Yes! It's a *ute!*" Chloe shouted.

"A what? A UFO?" Wendy dove to the floor of the Land Cruiser.

"Not a UFO! It's our *ute*. A *ute* is a pickup truck." Chloe laughed and pulled Wendy back onto the seat.

"It's Mummy and Dad. They have the *ute's* roof searchlight on." Jack laughed and then he hiccupped. That made Wendy and Chloe laugh until tears ran down their cheeks.

Wendy finally took a deep breath. "We're going to be okay. We're safe."

The blinding white light of the *ute* drew closer to the Land Cruiser. The kids could just barely make out the shapes of two adults.

Mr. and Mrs. Taylor pulled up beside them.

"We thought you were the Min Min lights," Jack said. He could hardly catch his breath.

"I think you've been alone in the dark too long, Jacko," Mrs. Taylor said, but she hugged him and sounded a little giddy herself.

Chloe's dad laughed and hugged Chloe and Jack. "And you must be Wendy." He stuck out his hand and Wendy shook it. "You're from San Francisco? I was there a long time ago. Beautiful city. And cold even in the summer! Welcome to our sheep station."

Wendy liked his friendly face and big smile. She could see where Chloe got her blue eyes. He had hair that might have been blond once and was still curly.

They transferred their bags to the *ute* and all five of them jammed into the cab. It turned out to be six bodies, though, because a bluish, short-haired dog with drooping ears stood on the seat in the cab.

"Buzz!" Chloe and Jack yelled.

Jack threw his arms around the dog.

He pulled Buzz onto his lap. "I've missed ya', *mate*." He rubbed the dog's ears and head.

Buzz licked Jack's face and then licked Wendy's face.

"He likes you, Wendy! Buzz doesn't like many people right away," Chloe said.

"I probably smell like granola bars," Wendy said.

Minutes later, they pulled up next to a sprawling one-story house. Even in the dark, Wendy could see it looked freshly painted and well cared for. Giant pots of red geraniums sat on each side of the wide steps. A broad porch wrapped the entire house. Wendy liked that. It would be slightly cooler somewhere every hour of the day.

"What a cool house," Wendy said. "I love the huge porch!"

"Porch?" Jack asked.

Mrs. Taylor tilted her head and thought a moment. "We call it a *verandah*," she said.

"Well," Wendy said. "I love the huge *verandah!*"

They unloaded the *ute*, and Mr. Taylor fired up the barbecue grill for dinner.

"Oh good! Throw another shrimp on the *barbie*," Wendy said. She was happy she could remember another Australian phrase.

"You want shrimp? You mean prawns?" Mrs. Taylor asked. She looked a little surprised.

Wendy's face got warm for a moment. "No, it's just something I've heard in the US. It was probably on a commercial."

"Well we're a long way from the ocean in the outback. But we do have lamb burgers," Mrs. Taylor said.

"You mean like hamburgers?" Wendy asked.

Chloe nodded. "Only better.

You'll see. It's best with a slice of beetroot on it."

"A slice of beet?" Wendy wrinkled up her nose. But it took only two bites for Wendy to agree. The lamb had a little different flavor, but the beet slice added a little sweetness. She liked it. Frankly, *anything* tasted better than granola bars these days.

Mrs. Taylor also set out potato salad and a green salad. So it didn't seem that different from an American barbecue.

After the kids dried the last of the dinner dishes, the adults shooed them off to bed.

Wendy changed into her nightgown and brushed her teeth. She felt like she'd already been in Australia a year even though it had only been less than a week.

The evening had exhausted the two girls. But they still had a drowsy conversation from their bunk beds.

"So do you really think the Min Min lights are UFOs?" Wendy asked.

"I don't know what they are. But something is

happening to the sheep." There was a long pause and Wendy thought Chloe had fallen asleep.

And then she said, "We've got to figure it out. The sheep station is already in bad trouble because of the drought. The *billabongs* are drying up."

"*Billabongs?*" Wendy asked.

Chloe nodded. "The ponds. The places where the sheep drink. That's awful enough. Losing sheep only makes it worse. Dad thinks he might need to start taking in tourists. But then it won't be a true station anymore. And tourists, well, they don't understand. They're here for a day or two and then they leave. How can they really know what station life is all about?"

Again, she paused for a long, long time. Wendy had fallen asleep when Chloe's voice woke her. "We've got to figure out what's going on before Dad loses the station."

Chapter 6

The Unhappy Surprise

The next day started hot and then it got hotter.

The girls sat on the west *verandah*, which was in the shade. It wasn't remotely cool. But a little breeze kept them from baking. They each had a bowl of Rice Bubbles cereal. The box looked just like a Rice Krispies box. It even had the snap, crackle, and pop guys on the front. Chloe's mom brought out thick, crumbly toast and jars of vegemite and peach jam. It looked like they might go the whole weekend and not have to eat a single granola bar. Wendy couldn't believe her luck.

Chloe put a thin layer of vegemite on her toast. "Try it. You'll like it," she said to Wendy.

Wendy sniffed the jar and spread a tiny bit of the brown goo on a corner of her bread. It tasted like yeast to her. She wrinkled her nose. "Thank you. But I think I'll have the jam instead."

In the daylight, Wendy could see that the station was far more than just a house or even a regular farmyard. Not that she'd seen a real farm in the US, but she'd seen pictures of farms. This looked more like a very small town. She counted at least twelve buildings. All of them had a fresh coat of white paint with red on the trim. The whole place looked tidy and clean. Happy.

One man in dusty jeans and a rumpled hat worked around the closest building with a shovel and wheelbarrow. Wendy could see he wore boots.

But she couldn't see if they were crocodile boots. Still, she wondered if the man was Rex, the *jackaroo*.

"Where are all the sheep?" Wendy asked.

"This time of year they're out in the *paddocks*."

"*Paddock?* What's that?" Wendy asked. "Is that like a pasture?"

Chloe tilted her head and thought a minute. "I think so. It's where the sheep graze. Dad and the *ringers* finished shearing them in October, just before the ewes started lambing." She looked at Wendy. "That means cutting the wool off before the mother sheep start having baby lambs. Now they're growing more wool." Chloe stopped crunching her cereal. "Or more likely growing wool and getting stolen." She sighed and shook her head. She dug into her cereal again.

The Unhappy Surprise

"Do you really think it's the Min Min lights?" Wendy asked. In the daylight, it seemed silly to think that lights could be scary. It seemed even sillier to think lights could steal sheep.

Chloe shrugged her shoulders and scrunched up her nose. "It seems crazy, doesn't it? But every time one of the *ringers* sees Min Min lights out on the land, sheep disappear." She went back to eating her cereal. "It's bad and getting worse," she said between bites. "A couple of the *ringers* have quit. They're afraid. And it's not easy to find people these days to work on a station. We're too remote."

"How many sheep have disappeared?"

Chloe paused and thought. "Maybe a hundred. I know that might not sound like a lot out of 10,000. But it's scary. If Dad can't figure it out, we could lose a whole lot more."

"And the Min Min lights always show up the same night?"

Chloe nodded. "And that's what's kind of crazy. Most people in the outback go their whole lives and never see the Min Min lights. And now people on the station have seen them six different times in a couple of months."

"Strange. Really, really strange." Wendy picked up the last of the toast crumbs with her finger. She was so thankful not to be picking up granola bar crumbs. She licked her finger and then stopped. Maybe licking your fingers was rude in Australia. But Chloe didn't seem to notice. Wendy picked up a few more crumbs.

Chloe gathered up her cereal bowl and glass. "Come on. I want to show you the most amazing place on the whole station. It's why I want to come back and live here some day."

The girls took their dishes into the kitchen. Chloe stopped by the back door and grabbed a tube of sunscreen. She put a glob on her hand and handed the tube to Wendy. "Gotta' be careful. The sun's a killer in the outback."

Wendy took the tube but laughed. "If I ever see the sun in San Francisco, I do a little dance."

"Yeah?"

"We live on the ocean side of the city. It's foggy way too much of the time."

"Well, it's never foggy in the outback." Chloe grabbed a sun hat from a hook by the door and handed it to Wendy. She took one for herself. She picked up two pairs of sunglasses (Chloe called them *sunnies*). She also took two wooden walking sticks and gave one to Wendy. "Snakes," she said.

"What do you mean snakes?" Wendy bit her nail.

"Well, if you see a snake, you have a stick to flick it away," Chloe said.

"Flick it away?" Wendy felt faint. If she *did* see a snake, she *would* faint. "I don't know if I'm cut out for this."

Chloe laughed. "Okay. Just pretend it's for walking. I'll flick the snakes."

They headed outside. The screen door slammed behind them. "Come on, Buzz." Chloe whistled for the dog. When he came, she scratched him behind the ears. "He'll scare the snakes away."

The girls paraded past the station buildings. Chloe named them as they passed. "This one is the shearing shed. They shear the sheep's wool off here in the spring. That one is the shearer's

quarters. The *ringers* live in this bunkhouse."

After they passed the last building, they turned right on a jeep path. Wendy kept to the middle where the grass was short. She kept her eyes on the taller grass on both sides of the path. If a snake darted out, she wanted to be ready to jump on the other side of Chloe.

Above them, a milky blue sky stretched forever. It met the red soil and the scrubby pale green bushes that covered the ground. A few dusty trees dotted the land. But mostly it felt wide open.

"When it rains, the land explodes with color," Chloe said. "All the wildflowers bloom. Birds come out. It's like the rain wakes them up." She poked a stick at the ground and knocked some red dust off the grass at the side. "The trouble is, it doesn't rain very often."

The night before, the land had looked dead. Now even in this blazing heat, Wendy could see lizards and critters and, yes, even a couple of snakes slither away. The snakes didn't have sticks, but they did seem even more nervous about the girls than the girls did about them. Wendy relaxed a tiny, tiny bit.

"Wendy, I don't know if you know it, but Mum, Jacko, and I just moved to town this summer. Up until now, we lived out here on the station."

"Really? But why did you move? Are your mom and dad, well are they . . ." She realized she shouldn't be asking such a question.

"Oh no. They're fine," Chloe said quickly. "We moved because Jacko is starting *kindy*. School is a real hassle out here on the station. I've had to do School of the Air."

"What's that?"

"I have class for an hour a day on the internet with my teacher. The rest of the day I do my homework. It's easier now than when my dad was my age. He listened to his teacher on a short-wave radio. He did his lessons and then mailed them in or sent them with the Royal Flying Doctor Service when they came through."

"That's really cool."

"Well, sometimes. Mostly, though, I miss playing with kids my own age." She looked at Wendy. "That's why I was so glad when you moved in next door. At least I'll know one person when I start school." She smiled big. "And I'm glad it's you that I know."

"Me, too!" Wendy truly was happy. It made her especially glad to know Chloe wouldn't stop being her friend when school started.

"We're almost there," Chloe said. "Close your eyes."

Wendy closed her eyes and Chloe took her arm. The girls rounded a red cliff and Chloe gasped.

"What's wrong?" Wendy asked and opened her eyes.

Chloe took a deep breath and pointed at a newly built structure. "That."

Wendy could only see a small group of trees. In the middle, a brand new platform stood about ten feet off the ground. The platform had a small cottage built on top. It reminded Wendy of a treehouse with an amazing view of the land for miles around. Beyond the trees, the land opened up into an enormous valley. Red bluffs and stands of trees dotted the open space. The view would be stunning.

Wendy still didn't get what had upset Chloe. "It looks like a really cool treehouse."

Chloe sighed a deep, sad sigh. "It's the first tourist cabin. They want to be out in the bush, but they don't want to have to worry about snakes or dingoes or anything."

"I still don't get it, Chloe. Why is it so awful to have tourists?" Wendy asked.

The Unhappy Surprise

Chloe just stared at the platform. "It just means that it's over. Dad's given up. He doesn't think the sheep station *can* survive." She wiped her cheeks. It was only then that Wendy realized Chloe had started crying.

"But if the tourists help bring in money, maybe the station can survive," Wendy said. She tried to be soft and kind in the way she said it. But Chloe just started crying harder and shaking her head.

"I don't expect you to understand. The station has been in my dad's family for five generations. This is all my dad's family has ever known. It's all I've ever known. And now it's gone." She sniffed and wiped her cheeks again. "Or it's almost gone. Now it'll just be a hotel."

Wendy felt sad for her new friend. And because Chloe was crying, Wendy felt like crying, too.

Chapter 7

Welcome to the Treehouse

"Do you think it would be okay to climb up and see what the treehouse looks like?" Wendy asked.

"Might as well," Chloe answered.

The girls opened the tall gate to the stairs and climbed up. A fancy wire mesh covered the stairway.

Chloe pointed to the wire mesh. "That should be good to keep the wild animals out. Dad thought of everything."

They stepped out onto a stained wooden deck.

It had a sharp smell of fresh lumber.

The view had been stunning from the ground. The view from here took Wendy's breath away. The deck hung over a cliff. When Wendy looked down, she couldn't see the land ten feet below her. Instead, she saw the bottom of the valley at least a hundred feet below her. She could faintly hear the baaing herds of sheep scattered over the valley. Wherever they grazed, the grass looked dusty green.

"I hate to say this, Chloe, but the tourists are going to go bonkers about this spot."

"Bonkers?"

"Crazy! They're going to love it! You could charge a mint for this place."

"A mint? Like peppermint?"

Wendy laughed. "Tons of money. Loads of money. Lots of money." She took in the full view and sighed. "Wow! Just Wow!"

Chloe smiled. "It is amazing, isn't it?" She relaxed a tiny bit.

"I know it makes you sad, Chloe, to bring tourists here. But think of it this way. The tourists will get to *be* in the outback. You'll be sharing something really special."

"True." But Chloe didn't sound convinced.

The girls peeked in the window of the little house. It had an overstuffed couch and chair and cozy kitchen table with two chairs. An eating bar separated the sitting area from the kitchen.

They could see a short refrigerator, narrow stove, and a metal sink. The cabinets above the sink had glass doors. Already someone had neatly stacked plates, cups, and bowls on the shelves. Behind the small kitchen, they could see another door and narrow stairs that led up to a loft. They could barely make out a bed at the edge of the loft. It had fluffy pillows and a downy yellow comforter on it.

"Hey, look at that." Chloe pointed at the ceiling of the loft. "It looks like there are huge skylights that have a shade over them. I'll bet you can pull the shade during the day to keep the heat out—"

"And open the shades at night to see the stars," Wendy finished.

"You can't believe the stars out here at night," Chloe said. "There aren't any city lights or even lights from houses. You can only see the moon and a sky full of stars."

"And Min Min lights," Wendy added.

The girls looked at each other. They looked at the treehouse. They looked out onto the wide open valley.

"Do you have the nerve?" Chloe finally asked.

"To watch for the Min Min lights from here?" Wendy asked. Her neck tingled. Her stomach did a somersault. She bit her nail.

Chloe nodded slowly.

Wendy took a deep breath. And then another.

And then one more. "Here's the funny thing. My Chinese name, Wen Chi? It means steady. But my mom says she wishes she would have given me a name that means brave instead. I don't know why. I'm never brave."

"What? I disagree." Chloe said firmly. "You were brave to come to Australia instead of staying in California. You were brave to come out to the sheep station even though you didn't really know us. You were brave to walk down the jeep path when you were worried about snakes. I think you're very brave."

"Really?" Wendy said. She thought about what her new friend said. She smiled. "Maybe. Maybe I am a little bit brave after all."

Chloe tilted her head slightly. "Here's the question. Are you going to be even braver tonight, Lee Wen Chi?"

Wendy paused a long time. She stared out over the open valley again. Her eyes took in the beauty.

Her head sorted out the risk. Finally, she said, "Yes. I'm going to be brave tonight."

"Me too," Chloe whispered.

Chapter 8

Settling In

It took less convincing than they expected. Chloe's dad had wanted the treehouse to be a surprise. Now that the girls had already seen it, Chloe's mom and dad agreed that family should be the first people to stay in the treehouse. Well, at least on the deck. They didn't want to risk getting the inside dirty. Chloe and Wendy even agreed that Jack could join them as long as he didn't talk too much.

"What do you want for your picnic dinner?"

Mrs. Taylor asked as she opened a picnic basket.

"Anything except granola bars and peanut butter sandwiches," Wendy said. She felt brave just for saying that, so maybe she could be brave if she needed to be. And then she saw Mrs. Taylor take a box of granola bars and a jar of peanut butter out of the picnic basket she was packing. So then she felt bad for being so rude.

"No, no, no. I'm sorry. I didn't mean to be rude. I'll eat anything. Really," she said.

"*No drama*, Wendy. You can't offend an Aussie. We say what we think all the time. Besides, you have the right idea. This should be a special picnic, not an ordinary one. Let me do some thinking. I'll make a little surprise and bring it out to you later. You kids pack up overnight bags and grab some *swags*."

"What's a *swag*?" Wendy asked.

Mrs. Taylor cocked her head and thought a moment. "I think you call it a sleeping bag."

Settling In

"Can we take Buzz?" Jack asked. He scratched the dog's ears.

"Sure. He'll be a good watchdog for you," Mrs. Taylor said.

"We need a watchdog?" Wendy asked Chloe as they packed. "For more than the Min Min lights?"

Chloe nodded her head carefully. "It *is* the outback. But we'll be fine. The gate and the wire mesh over the outside stairs will keep animals out. Buzz will scare away anything that comes close."

Wendy bit her nail.

"Really. We'll be fine," Chloe said again.

The three kids headed out on their adventure. They'd stuffed *swags* and sweatshirts into daypacks. They marched past the shearing shed and the shearer's quarters and the *ringers'* bunkhouse. Buzz trotted beside them. He stopped to sniff here and there. He lifted his leg and marked this spot and that. He could sense the adventure in the air, too.

"*Holy-dooly!* This place is great!" Jack shouted when he saw the treehouse. "I'm going to live here and never go back to the station."

Chloe laughed. "What are you going to eat?"

"I'll kill me some snakes and fry them up. And just in case, I'll bring some granola bars."

Wendy warned him, "You'll be disappointed."

The three of them laughed and climbed the stairs. Buzz raced up the steps then down the steps then up again. Even in the heat of the day, the deck felt comfortable. The roof covered the full deck and shaded it from the hot sun. A soft breeze blew through the space and cooled it further.

They pulled out their *swags* and sat on them. Jack handed out chewies to everyone. And Chloe brought out a deck of cards.

"Want to play Fish?" Chloe asked. She explained the rules to Wendy as she shuffled the deck.

"Easy peasy," Wendy said. "I know this game.

Settling In

It's like our game of Go Fish."

"Easy peasy?" Jack repeated. "You talk so funny." But from then on, every time he got a card from Chloe or Wendy, he said, "Easy peasy." And then he'd laugh and laugh.

Before they'd finished their tenth game, Mr. and Mrs. Taylor rolled up in the *ute*. Mrs. Taylor carried up a picnic basket while Mr. Taylor lifted four painted wood chairs and a table out of the back of the *ute*. All three kids, even Jack, helped carry them up to the deck.

"The paint wasn't quite hard on these yesterday. But this is it," he said. "Everything is finished."

"It's just as beautiful as you said, Steve," Mrs. Taylor said.

Mr. Taylor smiled. "We'll get a few tourists. We won't even know they're here." He tousled Chloe's curls. "So *no drama*, missy. *She's apples.*"

Chloe sighed.

"Let me show you around." Mr. Taylor unlocked the door and led them through the cozy place. It only took a few minutes because the treehouse wasn't very big. The best part was what Chloe and Wendy had already discovered. The shades above the bed pulled up and the sky filled the room.

"Ohhhhh," Mrs. Taylor said. "If I slept here, I might not ever sleep. Imagine all the stars you'd see."

"It'll get hot with it open, though." Mr. Taylor pulled the shades down again. "Okay, enough of the tour," he said and pecked his wife on the cheek. "I'm *hungry enough to eat a horse and chase the jockey.* Let's see what treats you packed for us."

Mrs. Taylor pulled out cold sodas for everyone.

Settling In

Next came out barbecued chicken (still warm!),
pasta salad, fruit salad, and lamingtons for dessert.
Wendy loved the little square cakes with chocolate
frosting and coconut on every single side.

"I made damper bread in the oven. Doing it over
a fire would have been more fun but a lot of work."

Chloe explained, "It's traditional bread. *Swagmen*
used to put the dough on a stick and roast it over an
open fire."

"Swagmen?" Wendy asked.

"They were people who wandered from place
to place," Mr. Taylor explained.

"I get it. The *swagmen* slept in *swags*," Wendy said.

"Exactly!" Chloe said.

"I'm *full as a goog*," Jack said and leaned back.
He patted his tummy and smacked his lips.

"DE-licious!" Wendy said. Secretly she
wondered if the Taylor family would notice if she
moved in with them. At least for meals. Maybe her

mom could move in, too. Who knew? She might even somehow learn to cook something.

Mrs. Taylor packed up the leftovers into the basket. She left a bag of apple scones and juice boxes on the table. "For *brekkie*. That's breakfast," she said and nodded to Wendy. And then she pulled out chocolate bars and more juices for the kids. "It's a special night, so you can have a midnight snack if you're hungry."

Mr. Taylor gave one more round of instructions about what they could do (go inside if it got cold or they had to use the *loo*).

Chloe whispered, "That means use the toilet."

And he told them what they should not do (use the bed or make a mess). And then Mr. and Mrs. Taylor hopped into the *ute* to drive back to the house. They disappeared into the dusky red evening.

And now the three of them and Buzz were alone in the outback

Chapter 9

The Duffers Arrive

"More cards?" Jack asked before the red dust settled behind the *ute*.

"Not now, Jacko," Chloe answered. "We need to have a plan for the night."

Wendy nodded. "It won't work if we get crazy scared like last night. We have to stay awake and watch for the Min Min lights."

"And watch for sheep disappearing," Chloe added.

"How are we going to do that? It's getting dark," Jack said. He sounded nervous.

"With these," Chloe said. She pulled binoculars out of her pack. "We can still see a lot now. When the moon comes up, we'll be able to see almost as much."

"We don't need light if the Min Min lights show up," Jack said. "Do you think we'll see them?" He pulled Buzz closer and rubbed the dog's neck.

"Jacko, if you get scared, you can sleep inside the treehouse on the floor." Chloe sounded gentle with her brother. "But if you stay out here, you have to be brave. Like Wendy and me."

He nodded solemnly.

"The Min Min lights are after the sheep. Not us," Wendy added.

"What if they get confused and think we're sheep? Chloe and me kind of have sheep hair." He ran his fingers through his blond curls.

The Duffers Arrive

"*No drama*, Jacko. We've got Buzz. He'll scare them off," Chloe said.

The three of them crawled into their *swags*. They rested their backs against the treehouse and watched the setting sun. Color spread across the sky.

"I missed seeing the sun set the last few weeks," Chloe said. "There are too many houses in the way in town."

"What a show!" Wendy got out her phone and took a picture. She looked at the result on her phone and sighed. "A photo can never, ever capture this."

"It's like this every night in the outback," Chloe said. She sounded happy. Contented.

"I never think about sunsets," Wendy said. "I don't ever see one in San Francisco. Sometimes we get nice colors in the sky. But unless I'm at the beach, I never see the sun drop like this."

"Sometimes after a really bad day, if I see a

good sunset, it makes everything better," Chloe said.

Just above the roof, something cackled. Wendy froze. "What's that sound?"

"That's just a kookaburra," Jack said. "They love gum trees."

"It sounds like it's laughing," Wendy said. She relaxed. A little.

"Are we going to stay up all night to watch for the Min Min lights?" Jack asked.

"I think we should," Chloe said. "We can take turns staying awake."

Below them in the valley a small herd of kangaroos hopped past. On the other side of the valley, a dingo howled.

Jack gasped softly.

"Chloe, will you stay awake with me when it's my turn?" Jack asked.

"Let's make your turn the first one," Wendy

said. "And all three of us will stay awake." She patted the space between Chloe and her. "Why don't you sleep in the middle, Jacko? We'll all be glad for Buzz if we get scared."

Jack let go of Buzz just long enough to tumble in between the two girls. "This is perfect," he said.

Chloe nodded. "Yes, it is, Jacko. Yes, it is."

Another dingo howled. The sun dipped below the horizon for good. Wendy felt Jack tense up. "I'm glad we've got Buzz and we're high up off the

73

ground," she said. "*She's apples*. We'll be fine."

Jack nodded and relaxed a tiny bit. "And snakes can't climb the stairs."

"Nope," Chloe said. "Besides, they all crawl into their dens at night."

The three of them talked about stuff. About school. About the things that made them nervous. About California. About being far from home. About not knowing what would happen if they lost the sheep station.

"Is your dad coming to Australia?" Jack asked at one point.

"Jacko!" Chloe said. "Don't ask things like that."

Wendy sighed. "No, no. It's okay that he asked." She never liked questions about her dad. She shook her head. "He died in a car accident when I was two. I don't remember him. I look at pictures of him holding me, but he's just a happy, friendly stranger."

The Duffers Arrive

"That's really sad," Chloe said. "I'm sorry Jacko asked you about your dad."

"It's okay. How could you know?" Wendy shrugged her shoulders. "The funny thing is that I don't miss him. But I do miss having a dad." She thought of Mr. Taylor and how he tousled Chloe's hair. "I know I'm missing something, and I don't even know what it is. Sometimes that's the hard part."

"You can share our dad, Wendy. He's a good *bloke*," Jack said.

"That's very generous of you, Jacko." Wendy smiled in the dark. "I'd like that. Especially here in Australia." She was lucky to have found friends like this so quickly. "In San Francisco, I have my *lao lao* and *lao ye* living nearby. That's my grandma and grandpa, my mom's parents. They take really good care of me when my mom is working. They're like a mom and dad in lots of ways. But they're old, you know? They don't ride bikes or play tennis in the park with me."

The three of them and even Buzz sat quietly for a few minutes. The final colors of the night shifted from purples and oranges into midnight blues and finally inky black. The stars popped out in the sky.

"Wow!" Wendy said. She could hardly breathe as she looked at the show. "This is . . . this is . . . I've never, ever seen anything like this." She looked at her friends in the dark. "What if I'd gone my whole life without seeing a sunset and sky like this?"

"See the Southern Cross constellation?" Chloe asked. She pointed to five stars in the shape of a kite. "It's what's on the Australian flag."

"What a cool thing to put on a flag," Wendy said.

A giant moon rose up through the hills to the east. It cast sharp shadows across the land.

The Duffers Arrive

A falling star streaked from nowhere to somewhere on the earth.

"Wow!" Wendy said softly again.

And then the dingoes started howling. Not just one, but a pack of them.

And the sheep started baaing and bleating.

Wendy's heart raced. She looked at Chloe, who had already jumped out of her *swag*. She leaned on the deck rail and focused the binoculars.

Wendy leaped out of her *swag*, too. "Over there!" She pointed across the valley. "That's where the noise is coming from." In the moonlight, they could see the sheep running like crazy in the field. They looked panicked. Two tiny headlights headed down a track and into the middle of the *paddock*.

"No! Over there!" Jack shouted. He pointed the opposite direction. Right where a giant bright light zoomed down off the cliff. And then it flew up again.

"A Min Min light!" Chloe yelled.

Chapter 10

The Duffers Attack

"Keep your binoculars on the sheep," Wendy yelled. "Something's happening. But I don't think it's the Min Min lights that are doing it." She yanked on her shoes and darted to the stairs.

"Where are you going?" Chloe asked.

"To the house. We've got to wake up your dad. He's got to get down to where the sheep are." Wendy's heart pounded. How could she run all the way back to the house in the dark?

"No! I should be the one to go!" Chloe grabbed her shoes.

The three of them froze for one second. And then Wendy gathered up every single ounce of courage she had. And a bit more. "No. You need to stay here with Jacko. You need to watch the *duffers* out there."

Chloe and Jack looked at each other. Chloe finally nodded. "Wait." Chloe grabbed her pack and dug out a flashlight. "Here's a *torch.*" She tossed Wendy the flashlight. Chloe swung the binoculars up to her eyes again and focused on the sheep.

Wendy clattered down the stairs. The light of the flashlight bounced ahead of her.

"And take Buzz!" Jack yelled after her. The dog scampered down the steps after Wendy. "He'll keep you safe."

Wendy took off running over the jeep trail. She hoped she was headed in the right direction.

The Duffers Attack

But she only had light from the moon and a *torch*, and everything happened so quickly. What if she'd gotten turned around? Buzz loved the run. He yapped loudly. Wendy worried he might nip her heels to go faster, but he just barked her on.

Just when she thought she couldn't run anymore, she saw the first building of the station. She pounded on. Her side ached and her legs ached and her lungs ached. She could hardly breathe. But she kept on running. She slowed only for a moment

when she rounded the corner and saw the dark station house. Buzz bolted ahead. He knew where to go.

Buzz yapped and yapped. He bounded up the *verandah* steps and raced back and forth.

A light flipped on. By the time Wendy made it to the steps, Mr. Taylor had made it to the screen door and was pulling on a shirt.

"What's happened?" he asked. Wendy heard the worry in his voice. "Are you okay? What are you doing here?"

"The Min Min lights. The sheep," Wendy said. She could hardly squeeze out the words. She leaned over to try to catch her breath. "You have to come. Fast."

Mr. Taylor raced to the *ute*. "Where? Which direction?"

Wendy jumped into the front seat, and Buzz scrambled up beside her on the seat.

The Duffers Attack

"That way," She pointed the direction to go. "We could see them from the treehouse."

Mr. Taylor took off the opposite way. "Don't worry. I know the *paddock*. This will be faster."

They bumped off of the main road and onto a rough, narrow track.

Wendy grabbed for a seatbelt only to find it stuck. She hung on to the door handle as if her life depended on it. She worried it did. They banged down a steep ravine and up a small hill. Wendy almost hit the *ute* ceiling as they jolted along. They flew past one *paddock* full of sheep and around a red cliff and onto another track.

"Wait!" Wendy yelled over the noise of the bouncing *ute*. "There was someone standing there. Right by the cliff."

"What? It's the sheep we're worried about," Mr. Taylor yelled back.

"But that's where the Min Min light dropped

to." Wendy pointed at the cliff. "If you find who is behind the Min Min light, you'll find the sheep."

He took his foot off the gas pedal and looked at her. "You're right. That's our *duffer*." He backed the *ute* around and bumped over the rough ground.

By the time they got to the cliff, the person had disappeared. But his station *ute* was still there. And so was the bungee cable that held the giant light. The Min Min light.

"Rex." Mr. Taylor sighed. "I should have figured it out. But now we know." He got out and took the keys out of the *ute*. "He'll have a bit of a hike out of here."

He turned the *ute* around and headed for the *paddock* of sheep at the far end of the valley. He turned his *ute* lights off. It made it much easier to surprise Rex's friends as they were loading sheep onto their *ute*.

The men scattered in the dark. "They won't get

far," Mr. Taylor said. He stepped out of his *ute* and pulled the keys to their *ute*. Then he carefully led the sheep down the ramp off the *ute* and back down to the *paddock*.

"Wendy," he said. "I don't know what they teach you in San Francisco, but here's an important lesson. If you're going to steal sheep, pull the keys out of the *ute* first."

Chapter 11

Saved!

Even though it was the middle of the night, the station was wide awake. The other *ringers* made their way to the house. Everyone gathered on the west *verandah* just off the kitchen. Each one had a story about Rex. But mostly they just shook their heads. "We thought something was fishy with Rex. But we couldn't ever prove it," the foreman said.

Mr. Taylor drove out to the treehouse and brought Chloe and Jack home.

Saved!

Mrs. Taylor made coffee and tea and somehow managed to bake fresh scones fast enough to feed everyone.

Poor Rex. He was limping down the station road to the main road as the police drove up. He tried to hide in the bush, but it wasn't hard to spot him. Especially because he got spooked by a snake den about the time the police car passed.

They arrested him and had a confession from him before they reached town. The police even got a bank account number. So even though the family wouldn't get all of their stolen sheep money back, they would get enough that Mr. Taylor could relax. A bit.

"You kids were brave and smart," Mr. Taylor said.

Chloe smiled at Wendy.

"It was especially scary to run all by yourself in the dark like that," Mrs. Taylor said.

"Buzz protected me," Wendy said. She couldn't quite believe she had run to the station in the middle of the night. It spooked her just to think about it.

"How did you know that wasn't a real Min Min light?" Jack asked.

Wendy thought for a moment. "I guess it's because it didn't exactly fit what you guys described. It dropped fast. But then it bounced up, like a ball."

"You thought fast, Wendy. If you hadn't run to the house, we never would have caught the *duffers*," Mr. Taylor said. "Rex was a pretty smart guy. He rigged up a powerful light on a bungee cord. He had someone drop the light from above. His whole plan was to distract everyone with the Min Min light while his gang stole sheep somewhere else. It already worked for him. And it would have worked again. Except you kids saw it all and acted fast. I'm really proud of you."

Saved!

"Dad," Chloe asked. "Does this mean we won't lose the station?"

He sighed. "Chloe, we still need rain. But for the moment, yes, we're okay."

"And the tourists and the treehouse?"

Mr. and Mrs. Taylor looked at each other and then looked at the kids. "Well, what do you think? We'll let you kids decide."

Chloe and Jack looked at each other. And then they looked at Wendy. Wendy who loved the colorful sunset and the stars in the sky and the wide open space.

Jack nodded to Chloe. She smiled and said, "I think we should share this amazing place. I think we should invite them to come."

Sneak Peek of Another Adventure
Mystery of the Troubled Toucan

Chapter One

Putt. Putt. Putt. Sputter. Putt. Putt. Sputter. Putt. Sputter. Sputter. Sput—

Sofia Diaz whirled around and peered over the side of the sputtering boat. The dark waters of the Rio Negro slowed down as they flowed past. Her dad had told her that the Rio Negro flowed together with the Rio Solimões to create the Amazon River in Manaus. Up river, where they were, she could really see why the Rio Negro was named after the color of the water and meant "black river." The waters looked blacker now, even threatening, as the boat sputtered and slowed to a stop.

"Um, Dad, did the boat just die?" She wouldn't be surprised. The old, run-down wooden boat had blue paint peeling off the sides and a makeshift tarp duct-taped to the top for shade.

"I'm sure it's nothing Sofie-Bear," Mr. Diaz said. That was her nickname. Sofie-Bear. Her mom said she cried so loud in the hospital nursery that all the nurses were afraid of her. A bear, they agreed. She didn't mind though. She loved that her long, straight, dark-brown hair and matching dark-brown eyes were just like a brown bear. Plus, bears were strong and tough, and so was she. She could clench her sturdy jaw and give a fierce growl when she wanted to. But right now she felt much less like a big, bold bear and much more like a tiny, timid mouse.

Squawk! Yelp! Yelp! Yelp!

Sofia jumped. She squinted, trying to find the source of the sound coming from the lush broad-leafed rainforest that lined the Rio Negro.

Her dad was looking toward the back of

the boat. She followed her dad's eyes. Hugo, the captain of the boat, yanked the motor's starter rope. Nothing. He slammed the motor with his rough hand and shook his head in disgust. Then he did it again— the rope *and* the slamming. Still nothing.

"Estamos presos." We're stuck. Hugo's lip curled up in a slight grin revealing yellow, cracked teeth. What was there to smile about when you were stuck on a broken boat in the middle of the Amazon?

Find out what happens to Sofia and Júlia in the Pack-n-Go Girls book, Mystery of the Troubled Toucan.

Meet More Pack-n-Go Girls!

Discover Brazil with Sofia and Júlia!

Mystery of the Troubled Toucan
Nine-year-old Sofia Diaz's world is
coming apart. So is the rickety old boat
that carries her far up the Rio Negro
river in Brazil. Crocodiles swim in the
dark waters. Spiders scurry up the twisted tree trunks.
And a crazy toucan screeches a warning. It chases Sofia and
Júlia, her new friend, deep into the steamy rainforest. There
they stumble upon a shocking discovery. Don't miss the
second Brazil book, *Mystery of the Lazy Loggerhead.*

Discover Austria with Brooke and Eva!

Mystery of the Ballerina Ghost
Nine-year-old Brooke Mason is headed to
Austria. She'll stay in Schloss Mueller, an
ancient Austrian castle. Eva, the girl who
lives in Schloss Mueller, is thrilled to meet
Brooke. Unfortunately, the castle's ghost
isn't quite so happy. Don't miss the second and third Austria
books: *Mystery of the Secret Room* and *Mystery at the Christmas Market.*

94

Meet More Pack-n-Go Girls!

Discover Mexico with Izzy and Patti!

Mystery of the Thief in the Night

Izzy's family sails into a quiet lagoon in Mexico and drops their anchor. Izzy can't wait to explore the pretty little village, eat yummy tacos, and practice her Spanish. When she meets nine-year-old Patti, Izzy's thrilled. Now she can do all that and have a new friend to play with too. Life is perfect. At least it's perfect until they realize there's a midnight thief on the loose! Don't miss the second Mexico book, *Mystery of the Disappearing Dolphin*.

Discover Thailand with Jess and Nong May!

Mystery of the Golden Temple

Nong May and her family have had a lot of bad luck lately. When nine-year-old Jess arrives in Thailand and accidentally breaks a special family treasure, it seems to only get worse. It turns out the treasure holds a secret that could change things forever!

What to Know Before You Go!

Where is Australia?

Australia is both a country and a continent in the Southern Hemisphere. It's often called an island country because it's the only country on the continent. As a country, it includes the island of Tasmania and other small islands. It's the sixth largest country in the world in area and is completely surrounded by water. But it has only about 23,000,000 people, so it's fifty-fifth in population. The country has only six states. The outback, which is a desert, covers much of the country. Australia became a country in 1901.

Facts about Australia

Official Name: Commonwealth of Australia
Capital: Canberra
Currency: Australian dollar
Government: Federal parliamentary constitutional monarchy. It's a commonwealth of England, so the Queen of England is also the Queen of Australia.
Language: English
Population: 23,130,000
Major Cities:

Sydney: 4,920,970   Melbourne: 4,529,496
Brisbane: 2,308,720   Perth: 2,039,193
Adelaide: 1,316,779

Traveling in Australia

Australia is an amazing place to visit. You can snorkel on the Great Barrier Reef, travel thousands of miles in the deserted outback, or explore stunning wildlife in Tasmania. And yes, you will see kangaroos and even wild camels as you drive. Over a million wild camels roam the outback! The country is almost as big as the US, so plan to fly from one corner to another. Or be ready to take lots of time to drive long stretches of empty road.

What to Expect for Weather

Australia's seasons are the opposite of ours. So when it's summer in the US, it's winter in Australia. This means that Christmas falls in the middle of the summer. In much of Australia, it can be hot, hot, hot in the summer. On the coast, it can be very rainy. In the northern part of the country, it stays fairly warm all year around. In other parts of the country, though, the temperature can drop to well below freezing. It can even snow!

What about the Min Min Lights?

The Min Min Lights are real. No one knows for sure exactly what causes them. They appear out of nowhere and can follow people for long stretches. People have seen them for more than one hundred years in the outback. There are even stories about people disappearing when they see the lights. But those are just stories. So if you're driving through the outback on a dark and lonely night, keep your eyes open. You never know what you'll see.

What Australians Eat

You'll find lots of familiar foods in Australia. They're probably best known for their *barbies*—that's barbecue. *Snags*, or sausages, are the most common. But they also eat lots of beef, lamb, chicken, and even kangaroo and emu. They also barbecue vegetables, which are yummy. This recipe for lamingtons is simple because it uses ready-made cake.

Recipe for Lamingtons

If you make this recipe, be sure you get an adult to help you.

Ingredients:

1 pound cake (or other premade cake)	2 tablespoons melted butter
4 cups confectioners' sugar	1/2 cup warm milk
1/3 cup cocoa powder	1 pound unsweetened dried coconut

1. Combine the sugar and cocoa powder. Add the melted butter and warm milk. Mix well. It should be thin enough to dip the cake squares into. But it shouldn't be so thin that all the icing runs off.
2. Cut the cake into cubes about 2" on all sides.
3. Use a fork and dip the cake into the icing. Roll the cake in the coconut. Set the pieces on a wire rack to dry.

Say It Like an Australian!

Both Australians and Americans speak English. But the two countries pronounce words in different ways. Australians also have lots of slang, or colorful ways, to describe things. You've already discovered some of this slang in *Mystery of the Min Min Lights*. For more fun examples, check out the Pack-n-Go Girls website: www.packngogirls.com.

English	Australian
Hello	G'day
How's it going?	'Ow yar goin'?
Gum	Chewie
Wow!	Crikey!
Mad	Cross as a frog in a sock
Candy	Lollies
Tell on you	Dob on you
Kindergarten	Kindy
Thief	Duffer
Ranch or Farm	Station
Sidewalk	Footpath
Teasing	'aving a go
No worries	No drama
It's fine	She's apples

English	Australian
Australian cowboy	Ringer
Male station hand	Jackaroo
Female station hand	Jillaroo
Genuine	Ridgy didge
Pickup truck	Ute
Porch	Verandah
Pond or small lake	Billabong
My goodness!	Holy dooley!
Eaten too much	Full as a goog
Breakfast	Brekkie
Bathroom	Loo
Man	Bloke
Pasture	Paddock
Barbecue	Barbie
Sausage	Snag
Kangaroos	'Roos
Sunglasses	Sunnies
Flashlight	Torch
Sleeping bag	Swag
Someone who wanders	Swagman
Someone who talks a lot	Earbasher
Kilometers	Clicks
The truth	Good oil
Friend	Mate (Boy) or Love (Girl)

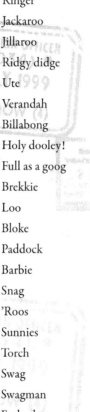

G'day!

My
Australian
Trip
Planner

Where to go: _____

_____

_____

_____

_____

_____

_____

_____

_____

_____

_____

_____

_____

_____

_____

What to do:

_____

_____

_____

_____

_____

_____

_____

_____

_____

_____

_____

_____

_____

_____

My Australian Trip Planner

Things I want to pack:

_____

_____

_____

_____

_____

_____

_____

_____

_____

_____

_____

_____

Friends to send postcards to:

_____

_____

_____

_____

_____

_____

_____

_____

_____

_____

_____

_____

Thank you to the following Pack-n-Go Girls:

Maia Caprice
Keira Clotfelter
Elizabeth De Pry
Lisa Muehlfellner
Sarah Travis

Thank you also to Maria Wen Adcock, Evelien Hayning,
Katherine Kates, Angela Lee, Stephen Martyn, and
Giselle Shardlow.

*And a special thanks to my Pack-n-Go Girls co-founder,
Lisa Travis, and our husbands, Steve Diller and Rich Travis,
who have been along with us on this adventure.*

Janelle Diller has always had a passion for writing. As a young child, she wouldn't leave home without a pad and pencil just in case her novel hit her and she had to scribble it down quickly. She eventually learned good writing takes a lot more time and effort than this. Fortunately, she still loves to write. She's especially lucky because she also loves to travel. She's explored over 45 countries for work and play and can't wait to land in the next new country. It doesn't get any better than writing stories about traveling. Janelle and her husband split their time between a sailboat in Mexico and a house in Colorado.

Adam Turner has been working as a freelance illustrator since 1987. He has illustrated coloring books, puzzle books, magazine articles, game packaging, and children's books. He's loved to draw ever since he picked up his first pencil as a toddler. Instead of doing the usual two-year-old thing of chewing on it or poking his eye out  with it, he actually put it on paper and thus began the journey. Adam also loves to travel and has had some crazy adventures. He's swum with crocodiles in the Zambezi, jumped out of a perfectly good airplane, and even fished for piranha in the Amazon. It's a good thing drawing relaxes his nerves! Adam lives in Arizona with his wife and their daughter.

Pack-n-Go Girls Online

Dying to know when the next Pack-n-Go Girls book will be out? Want to learn more Australian slang? Trying to figure out what to pack for your next trip? Looking for cool family travel tips? Interested in some fun learning activities about Australia to use at home or at school while you are reading *Mystery of the Min Min Lights*?

- Check out our website:
  www.packngogirls.com
- Follow us on Twitter:
  @packngogirls
- Like us on Facebook:
  facebook.com/packngogirls
- Follow us on Instagram:
  packngogirlsadventures
- Discover great ideas on Pinterest:
  Pack-n-Go Girls

Made in the USA
Middletown, DE
11 September 2018